Breaking Free
A university diary: Book 1

Level: 4/CEFR A2/800 headwords

By Paul McAleese

Edited by Craig Boobyer

Contents

The main characters

1. Late again?
2. The professor
3. A busy pizza shop
4. The café chat
5. A beach party
6. Mr. Right?
7. A fresh start
8. The competition

Appendix A: Key vocabulary & phrases

Appendix B: Key vocabulary & phrase mini-test

Appendix C: Mini-test answers & discussion questions

The main characters

Ria
A university student who wants to become a designer

Lucy
Ria's friend at university

Shelly
Ria's friend and classmate at university

Mr. Read
Ria's manager at her part-time job

Lockie
An international student at Ria's university

1. Late again?

It was already eight thirty. Ria was late again. Her class started at nine. She quickly got out of bed and took her phone and bag into the kitchen. Her mother was cooking breakfast.

"Do you want something to eat?" asked her mother.

"No, I have to go," said Ria.

"I hope you're not missing classes again," her father said. He was reading the newspaper at the kitchen table. "We pay a lot of money for you to go to university."

"Sorry Dad, no time. I'm late for class!" said Ria.

"I cooked pancakes…" her mother started, but Ria had already left. She had to get to class quickly. Today was the last day for her homework **assignment**.

Ria ran to the apartment building elevator. She pushed the down button. She was sleepy. She often sends texts to her friends late at night. Ria checked her phone as she walked into the elevator. There was a short old man standing in the elevator. She almost walked into him.

"Watch where you're going young girl!" the old man shouted. He looked angry. He stamped his walking stick on the floor. "You young kids. Always looking at your smartphones. Look up more!" he said.

Ria tried not to look at him. She wanted to get out of the elevator quickly.

"When I was a kid, we never…" the old man said, as the elevator arrived at the first floor. Ria was already running out.

Ria took the bus to university. She thought about what her father said. Her parents were paying for her university courses. They wanted her to take business courses, but she didn't like them. She wanted to study design, but her father said business courses would help her find a good job.

Ria put on her headphones and played some music. It was a song she liked. It helped her to relax. She listened to the words in the song. 'Looking for my sunshine… Looking for my moonlight… Things are gonna get right…' She tried not to think about her assignment.

When Ria arrived at university, the class had already started. It was too late. The students had to give the **professor** their assignments at the beginning of class. *What am I going to do?* thought Ria. She decided not to go to the class. Instead, she went to the university **cafeteria**.

She liked the cafeteria. It had big windows and a beautiful view of the university lake and park. It also had better food than the other shops at the university. She liked to **hang out** there with her friends. Ria bought a coffee and sat down at an empty table.

"Hi Ria. What's up?" someone said.

Ria looked up to see her friend Lucy. Lucy was holding a plate full of food.

"Late breakfast?" Ria asked. Lucy was always eating.

"Ah…no. I ate breakfast earlier. This is an early lunch," Lucy laughed. She sat down and started eating.

"Wow! Who's that?" Lucy said suddenly.

"Where?" asked Ria.

"Over there!" she answered, looking at a group of people. "The tall guy in the dark brown sweater. He's cute!"

Ria looked at him. He was tall but not too skinny. He was also well dressed. She watched him talking to some other students. *Nice smile too,* Ria thought.

Beep-bum! The sound of Ria's phone surprised her. She took her phone from the table. It was a text from one of her other friends.

"Who's that?" asked Lucy through a mouth full of food.

"Hang on," said Ria as she answered the text. *Beep-bum* went her phone again. It was from a different friend. Suddenly Ria was busy texting. When she finished, she looked at the group of people again. She couldn't see the tall man. He had gone.

"Looking for **Mr. Right**?" Lucy smiled, "He left. Actually, he was looking at you when he walked out."

"Really? Was he looking at me?" asked Ria. *Who was he? Was he in any of her classes?* Ria thought.

"You **broke up** with Ken six months ago. It's time for you to find a new boyfriend," said Lucy.

Ken was Ria's boyfriend from high school. They broke up when she went to university.

"No. No. No. He's not my type," said Ria. But she was still thinking about him. *Will I see him again?* she thought.

2. The professor

"Your first year is not going well," Ria's professor said. "I'm sorry, but I cannot take late homework assignments, it's not fair to the other students," he explained.

Ria was now wishing she hadn't visited her professor's office. She still wanted to give her assignment to the professor, but he wouldn't take it.

"And there's one more thing," the professor said.

"What's that?" she asked.

"This is the second time you haven't done your assignment," he said. "You may not pass this course."

"Uh…really?" Ria said. She felt terrible. "Then what will I have to do to pass?" she asked.

"Well, you need to come to class more. You also need to stop talking to your friends and using your phone in class," he answered. "If you don't pass this course, you'll have to take it again next year."

"I see. I'm sorry. I'll try to work harder," said Ria. She was worried now.

"I hope to see you in class again on Monday," he said.

Ria left the professor's office. *Oh no!* she thought. *What am I going to tell my father if I don't pass my courses? I don't want to **drop out**.* She wanted to pass the business courses. She wanted to make her parents happy. But she also wanted to study the things she liked. She was nineteen now. She had her own dreams.

Ria thought about her future. She had loved drawing and art since she was a child. She joined the art club in high school. Later, she became interested in design. She also liked to make pictures and posters using software on her computer. She dreamed of having a job designing websites and advertisements. *That's the kind of job I want to do,* she thought. But she also worried about not having a job in the future.

Beep-bum! It was Ria's phone again. She looked at her phone. It was her classmate Shelly.

"Want to hang out after classes today?" asked Shelly's text.

"I have my part-time job after my classes. But I finish at five. How about after that?" Ria answered.

"Sure. Then how about meeting at Zack's around five thirty?" Shelly wrote.

"Sounds good," answered Ria. Zack's was a popular café in the downtown area.

"**Awesome**!" wrote Shelly. "See ya there."

"Sure. See ya later," answered Ria.

3. A busy pizza shop

Ria's part-time job was at a pizza shop. She took orders and helped make the pizzas. She didn't like her job. There were never enough staff at the shop. The phone was always ringing. She often hurt her hands on the hot pizza plates. Also, she didn't like the manager, Mr. Read. He always **picked on** her. 'You're late again!', 'stop checking your phone!' he would always shout at her.

Ria finished her work at five o'clock and got ready to leave the shop. Her manager, Mr. Read, suddenly asked to talk to her. *Oh no!* she thought.

"Before you go, I want you to take out the **rubbish**," said Mr. Read.

"It's already five o'clock and I have plans," said Ria.

"Taking out the rubbish is part of your job," said Mr. Read. "Stop talking and just do it!" he shouted.

Ria looked sadly at the mountain of rubbish bags in the corner of the shop.

"You damn students are all so lazy. You don't know how to

work hard," Mr. Read said.

Ria walked to the rubbish bags and started taking them outside. Mr. Read didn't help her. Instead, he just stood and watched her do it.

After leaving her part-time job, Ria took the bus downtown. She was already tired. The bus was crowded so she had to stand. She was late again. She hoped Shelly would still be waiting for her. Ria thought about her part-time job. She wanted to **give up** her job, but she needed money. She needed money to go shopping. She needed money to go out with her friends. She also needed money to pay her phone bill every month.

From the bus window Ria could see a lot of people on the streets. Her university was in a place called Hamilton. It wasn't the largest city in New Zealand, but the downtown area was often busy. She looked at her phone. She opened her favourite online shopping app. She started looking at some handbags she liked. She wanted to buy a new one, but they were expensive.

Ria noticed that her bus had arrived at the downtown bus stop. She quickly got off the bus. She had almost missed her stop. She ran across the street before the traffic lights changed. She walked quickly to the café. It was starting to rain. She looked at the shopping app on her phone again.

Suddenly, Ria looked up to see something quickly coming towards her. It was a man on a bicycle! The bicycle turned quickly but it was too late. The bicycle hit her hand and sent her phone flying onto the street. Ria let out a surprised scream. Her phone made a loud sound as it hit the wet street.

"Hey!" Ria shouted at the man. But he didn't stop. He kept riding.

"No, no, no!" Ria said. She picked up her phone. It was wet and the screen was broken. She tried to turn on the phone. Nothing. She tried again. Still nothing. *No way!* She thought. She sat down on the side of the street. She put her head in her hands. *What will I do without my phone!* she thought. She couldn't text her friends. She didn't have enough money to buy a new one. She then started thinking about the business courses she didn't like. She also started thinking about the part-time job she didn't like. *Nothing is going right!* she thought. *Can things get any worse?*

4. The café chat

Ria finally arrived at Zack's café. Her friend Shelly was drinking coffee at a back table. Shelly was in the same business course as Ria. After starting the course, they quickly became good friends. Shelly lived in the university **dormitory**. Ria also wanted to live there. Many students lived in the dormitory. She didn't like living with her parents.

"Hiya!" said Shelly as she pushed a chair out for Ria.

"Hi," answered Ria. She looked at Shelly's phone on the table.

"What's wrong?" asked Shelly.

"I can't believe it. It's my phone. It's broken," said Ria. "Someone on a bicycle hit me and I dropped it. The screen is broken. It won't turn on," Ria said, showing Shelly the broken phone.

"Oh no! That's terrible!" said Shelly. "Maybe you can get the person to pay for it?"

"No, he didn't even stop after hitting me," said Ria looking very sad, "but I was looking at my phone while walking. I should've been watching the street."

"Oh, I see," said Shelly.

Beep-bum! The sound came from Shelly's phone.

"Oh, a text," said Shelly. "You know what? I'm not gonna use my phone now. I'm gonna turn it off and put it in my bag. Let's make this a phone-free time," said Shelly.

"Oh thanks!" said Ria.

After that, Shelly and Ria had a great time at the café. They drank coffee, ate cake, and laughed together without their phones. They talked about TV dramas, movies, and fashion.

Later they talked about their plans for the weekend.

"Hey, wanna come to a beach party on Saturday?" asked Shelly, "Lucy's coming too. It's a big party. There'll be a lot of other students there. There'll also be **fireworks**."

"What a great idea!" said Ria. Ria loved watching fireworks. *Shelly's such an awesome friend,* she thought.

Ria took the bus home. She was happy to find a seat. She

looked at the large brightly-coloured advertisements in the bus. *I want to design those in the future,* she thought. She took a notebook from her bag and started drawing a picture. She imagined she was designing an advertisement.

While she was drawing, Ria thought about her day. She had the assignment problem. She got picked on at her part-time job. She also broke her phone. Then she decided not to think about her problems. She was **looking forward to** the beach party. She thought about the other students who might be there. Ria had made a lot of new friends since starting university. She didn't like her business courses but she enjoyed university life. It was more interesting than high school. She could meet more new and interesting people.

5. The beach party

On Saturday afternoon, Ria, Shelly, and Lucy decided to meet at the university bus stop. They would then go to the beach together. Ria was worried because her phone was broken. They couldn't contact her if their plans changed. But she didn't need to worry. When she got to the bus stop, Lucy had already arrived.

"Wow, you're not late for once," said Lucy.

"What's up?" Ria asked. She could see that Lucy was upset about something.

"I sent you about ten texts yesterday," said Lucy. "You didn't even answer one."

"Ohhhh. I broke my phone yesterday," said Ria. She now understood why Shelly was upset.

"Nice try. Everybody says that when they don't answer texts," said Lucy. She didn't believe Ria's story.

"No, I really did!" said Ria. She was laughing now, and Lucy started to smile too. "I don't know what I'm going to do. I don't have enough money to buy a new one. Anyway, it's only a phone I guess," Ria explained.

"What!" said Lucy, still smiling. "Everybody must have a smartphone!"

Later, Shelly and some other friends arrived. Soon, they all got on the bus and left for the beach. They talked and laughed together on the bus.

After a while, Shelly put on her headphones and Lucy started texting on her phone. Ria didn't have her phone, so she had nothing to do. She decided to look out the bus window. She thought about what Lucy said earlier. She worried about not having her phone. She couldn't answer her friend's texts. She heard some of her other friends were also upset with her. Ria tried not to think about it. The bus was now driving through the green countryside outside Hamilton. It was a nice view. It was a beautiful sunny day.

They arrived at the beach. There was a big group of young people laughing, eating, and drinking. They sat down on the beach together. They took out some drinks and started talking. Lucy had brought a lot of snacks. Ria opened her bag and took out her hat and sunglasses.

Shelly saw something in her bag. It was the advertisement

Ria drew while on the bus.

"What's that?" asked Shelly.

"Oh, it's nothing," said Ria. "Just something I drew the other day."

"It's awesome!" said Shelly. "You're really good at drawing. I'm **impressed**."

"Really?" said Ria, surprised. She looked at her drawing again. *Maybe Shelly's just trying to be nice,* she thought.

"Look!" Lucy said suddenly, "It's Mr. Right again. Over there!" she said, looking at a group of boys.

"Mr. Right?" asked Shelly.

"Yeah. Ria **has the hots for** him," said Lucy laughing.

"No way!" said Ria, "I don't have the hots for him. I haven't even met him." But she was excited he was there.

"Let's say hi to him," said Lucy. She put her hand up and shouted "HEEYYY!" to the group of boys.

"Stop it!" said Ria, pulling Lucy's hand down. "It's not funny," she said with a big smile.

"Huh? You ARE interested in him," said Shelly looking at Ria.

"Well. He is kinda cute," said Ria. The girls all laughed together.

"Can I have some more of that chocolate?" Ria asked Lucy. She was getting **embarrassed** and wanted to talk about something different.

"Are you girls also at Waikato?" somebody suddenly asked. Waikato was the name of their university. Surprised, the girls all looked up to see Mr. Right. He was standing in front of them.

"Sure are," Lucy quickly said, "and Ria here wants to be in your class!" she said laughing.

"Really?" Mr. Right asked, smiling at Ria. *There's that nice smile again. Perfect teeth too,* Ria thought.

"Well, actually… we are already in the same class," he said.

"Really?" Ria asked, surprised.

"But you're always on your phone, you probably haven't seen me," he said.

Ria also noticed he had an **accent**. He didn't sound like a New Zealander.

"Where are you from?" she asked.

"Bryant Hall dormitory," he answered, smiling.

"No, I mean…" Ria started.

"Liverpool, England," he answered before Ria could finish. "I'm Lockie. Nice to meet you."

"Same here. I'm Ria from the beach," she said. She decided to joke too.

"Nice to meet you Ria. You have a wonderful beach," smiled Lockie.

"And these are my friends Lucy and Shelly," said Ria.

"Nice to meet you all," said Lockie. "Hey, I'm really sorry. The boys over there are calling me back. I'll see you again in class," said Lockie.

"Sure," said Ria. Her heart was racing.

After it got dark, some of the groups on the beach let off fireworks. Ria enjoyed watching their bright colors in the dark night sky. She wanted to paint a picture of them. Ria saw that Lucy and Shelly weren't watching the fireworks. They were busy texting on their phones.

6. Mr. Right?

On Monday Ria went back to her business class. She sat down and took her books out.

"Is this seat taken?" asked Lockie, suddenly standing beside her.

"Sorry, my friend's sitting here," Ria said, looking up at him. "I'm just joking. It's not taken," she said with a smile. She was happy Lockie asked to sit next to her.

But they didn't talk at all in the class. Lockie was listening to the professor carefully. He was also taking notes. He didn't check his phone once. Ria was impressed. She also did her best to listen and take notes.

After the class, Ria and Lockie walked around the university lake together. It was a small lake, but it was nice and quiet. It was next to some trees and a big green grass area.

"Do you like living in New Zealand?" Ria asked.

"I love it here. I love the clean air. I love the mountains," Lockie answered, "I'm a real nature person. I love hiking."

"Me too," said Ria, looking at some ducks swimming on the lake.

"You didn't use your phone in class today. Did you forget to bring it?" asked Lockie.

"Actually, it's broken," said Ria.

"Oh, no," said Lockie. "But maybe that's not a bad thing."

"Really? Some of my friends are angry because I haven't answered their texts," said Ria.

"Don't worry about them. Real friends won't get angry if you don't text them back quickly. There are more important things in life than texting," said Lockie. "Because of your texting, you didn't even know I was in your class," said Lockie, smiling.

"Yeah," said Ria.

"So, what will you do after you **graduate**?" Lockie asked.

"I dunno. I'm interested in design, but my parents want me to study business. I like university, but I'm not interested in business. But I don't want to drop out," explained Ria.

"Design sounds interesting," said Lockie. "Web designers make a lot of money in my country."

"I don't think there are many good design jobs in New Zealand," said Ria.

"Don't give up on your dream," smiled Lockie. "You'll find a way," he said.

"My dad always says, 'where there's a will, there's a way'," he added.

"Where there's a will, there's a way?" asked Ria.

"Yeah, it means if you really want to do something, you will find a way to do it. But you have to work hard. And you can't give up," said Lockie.

After finishing their walk, they sat down in the big green grass area. They talked while watching the ducks in the lake. They talked about their interests. They also talked about their dreams for the future. Ria enjoyed talking with Lockie. She never talked like this with her ex-boyfriend Ken. Ria really liked Lockie. She liked his English accent too.

After saying goodbye to Lockie, Ria went to her part-time

job at the pizza shop. It was busy again. There were a lot of pizza orders. Her manager, Mr. Read, picked on her again. But Ria worked hard. She felt better about working today. She thought about what Lockie had said. *Where there's a will, there's a way,* she thought. If she worked more, she could get more money. Then maybe she could pay for a design course.

7. A fresh start

After finishing her part-time job, Ria went home. Her mother was cooking dinner. Her father was watching the evening news on TV.

"Did you take your broken phone to the shop?" her father called from the sofa.

"Yeah. They can't repair it. They said I needed to buy a new one. But I don't have any money," said Ria. She looked at her father hopefully.

"Well, we need to be able to contact you," her father said. "You'll also need a phone when you start working in business," he said. He looked at her over the top of his glasses. Ria tried not to listen too much.

"It doesn't need to be an expensive one. I'm going to use it less than my other phone," said Ria. Her mother and father looked at each other in surprise.

"Is this really Ria we are talking to?" her mother asked. "The Ria who loves to text her friends all the time?"

"This is the new Ria," she said.

The next day, Ria went back downtown and bought a new phone. She used money her father gave her. It was a warm sunny day, so Ria decided not to take the bus. Instead, she walked to her university. On the way, she sat down in a small park. She looked up at the top of a tree to see some birds singing. *That's beautiful,* she thought, *I need to look up more.*

Then she then took out her old phone. She looked at the broken screen. *From now, I'm going to do less texting,* she thought. *I'm going to use my time to work harder. I'm even going to study more in my business class. Then I'll find a way to study design. I'm going to follow my dream. This is the first stage in becoming the new Ria.* She then threw her old phone into a rubbish bin. She wrote a short text to Lucy and Shelly.

"Hiya. I now have a new phone. This is my new number and address," she wrote.

"But this is the new Ria. She will be doing less texting and more studying," she wrote and then added an emoji '☺.'

"See you girls at university tomorrow!" she wrote and then pressed send.

But Ria was worried about not texting her friends as much.

She worried about what they might think of her.

The next day she saw Shelly in class. Shelly was now sitting near the front. Ria walked over to her.

"I saw your text," said Shelly. "I've decided that I'm going to do less texting too," she said smiling. "I've even put my phone away and turned off the sound," said Shelly, looking at her jeans pocket.

Ria was happy that Shelly agreed with her new plan. They both listened carefully and took a lot of notes in the class. She noticed that Lockie wasn't in class. She had been looking forward to seeing him. *Is he okay?* she thought.

8. The competition

The next day Ria woke up early. Because she wasn't texting her friends late at night, she could sleep well. She got an early bus to university. She went to the university library to study. It was quiet. She was able to study for two hours without a break.

"Hi," said Lockie. Ria looked up and was surprised to see him standing there.

"Hi," said Ria. She was happy to see him.

"**Hitting the books**?" he asked.

"That's right," she answered. "I have to study more, but our class starts soon."

"Wanna walk there together?" asked Lockie.

"Sure," said Ria. She stood up and put her books in her bag. "You missed class yesterday," said Ria.

"I had to go to the dentist," said Lockie. He then opened his mouth to show a broken tooth. "I did it at rugby practice. I have to go to the dentist again next week. They said I need a new tooth," he explained.

"Oh, that must hurt," said Ria.

"Anyway, are you busy this weekend?" asked Lockie.

"No plans, just my part-time job on Sunday," said Ria. *Is he going to ask me out?* she thought.

"Wanna go to a movie?" asked Lockie.

"Are you asking me out on a date?" asked Ria, smiling at Lockie.

"No, ahh…maybe…ahh," said Lockie, his face turning red. He looked embarrassed. "Yes," he said looking at Ria.

"That would be great," said Ria.

Yes! thought Ria. *He's finally asked me out*. She was very excited. They walked to class together.

After class, Lockie had to go back to the library, so Ria went to the university cafeteria. She saw Lucy sitting at a corner table. Ria walked over and sat with her. Lucy was eating a lot again.

"Hiya," said Lucy. "Want some of my chicken salad bagel? I have two," she said.

"I'm okay," said Ria. "Early dinner?" Ria asked, smiling.

"Ahh…second lunch," answered Lucy laughing.

At that moment Shelly came to their table. She was holding a coffee.

"Hi girls," she said as she put her coffee on the table. Ria waited for Shelly to sit down before telling them both the good news.

"Guess who asked me out on a date?" said Ria.

"Mr. Right asked you out!" shouted Lucy. It even surprised the students at other tables.

"Keep it quiet," said Ria, smiling but very excited. "He has a name, Lockie, remember?" said Ria.

"I'm so happy for you," smiled Shelly.

"Me too!" said Lucy taking another big bite of her chicken salad bagel.

"That's great news. I was worried about you after you broke up with Ken," Shelly said. "I like Lockie. He's cute. He looks kind too. It's great that you guys are together now," said Shelly.

"Well, we're not together yet. He's only just asked me out," said Ria.

After the girls said goodbye to each other, Ria decided to go home. While walking to the bus stop alone, she passed the university notice board. She saw a large notice with 'Design Competition' written at the top. She stopped and read the notice. It was a competition to design a new cover for the university magazine. The winner would get a $500 prize. *This looks interesting,* she thought. *Maybe this could be my chance to design something? Maybe then my parents would let me take a design course.* She wrote down the email address on the notice.

After getting on the bus, Ria put on her headphones and listened to some music. She played her favourite song again. She listened to the words of the song. 'Looking for my sunshine…Looking for my moonlight…Things are gonna get right…' *Are things gonna get right for me?* she thought. She smiled to herself. Things were starting to get better in her life now. She was looking forward to the design competition. She was also looking forward to her date with Lockie on the weekend.

When Ria arrived at home, she walked into the elevator and pushed the button for her floor. Just as the doors were closing, a short old man with a walking stick entered the elevator.

Oh no! It's that angry old man again! thought Ria.

He looked at her. She looked at him.

Ria decided to smile.

"Hello," said Ria.

"Good afternoon young lady," the old man smiled back.

Appendix A: Key vocabulary & phrases

Key vocabulary	Meaning	Example
accent (n)	The different way a person from another country (or area) speaks, especially their pronunciation	The new student spoke with an Australian **accent**.
assignment (n)	Work that somebody must do, usually as part of their study or job	Jane couldn't go to the party because she was busy doing her history class **assignment**.
awesome (adj)	Great; excellent	I just bought this **awesome** new computer game!
break up (pv)	End a relationship (past=broke up)	I think Richard will **break up** with Jane soon. I don't think they like each other anymore.
cafeteria (n)	A place where people can buy and eat food, usually at a	The university **cafeteria** is located on the

	school or large company	second floor of building C.
dormitory (n)	A building for university students or company staff to live in (=dorm)	Do you live in the university **dormitory** or your own place?
drop out (pv)	Leave school or university before finishing your studies	Jerry found school too difficult so he decided to **drop out** and look for a job instead.
embarrassed (adj)	Feel shy or uncomfortable about something	I was **embarrassed** when the teacher told the class my test score.
fireworks (n)	Things that are launched into the sky and explode to make bright colors; often used at large outdoor festivals and celebrations	People in many countries like to let off **fireworks** to celebrate the New Year.
give up (pv)	Stop trying to do something, usually	Betty had to **give up** playing tennis

	before it has been completed (=quit) (past=gave up)	on the weekends because she was too busy with work.
graduate (v)	Complete all of a university or high school program and receive some kind of certification or degree/diploma	Sam was planning to **graduate** from university soon, so he started looking for a job.
hang out (pv)	Spend time relaxing in a place or with another person (past=hung out)	Simon likes to **hang out** with his friends after rugby practice.
have the hots for (i)	Have a romantic interest in somebody	Simon **had the hots for** his classmate, but he was too shy to talk to her.
hit the books (i)	Study a school or university subject very hard	My tests start next week. It's time to **hit the books**!
impressed (adj)	Have a feeling of respect or admiration for somebody.	I was **impressed** by how much Keiko's English had improved.

look forward to (pv)	Be happy thinking about something that is going to happen	Jack is **looking forward to** the summer holidays. He has planned a trip to Canada.
Mr. Right (n)	A man who would make the perfect/ideal boyfriend or husband	I'm not going to rush to get married, I'm going to wait until **Mr. Right** comes along.
pick on (pv)	Bully or tease somebody; treat someone unfairly or badly	You shouldn't **pick on** people just because they're different.
professor (n)	A kind of teacher at a university	Dr. Jones was one of my **professors** at university.
rubbish (n)	Things that you throw away because you no longer need them (US English=trash)	The **rubbish** in our neighborhood is collected every Thursday.

n=noun, v=verb, adj=adjective, pv=phrasal verb, i=idiom

Appendix B: Key vocabulary & phrase mini-test

Choose the most correct answer

1. Richard didn't like school when he was a child because the other kids used to _____ on him.
   A. give up   B. hit the books   C. drop out
   D. pick on

2. Because her grades were poor, Sally _____ of university and found a job.
   A. gave up   B. broke up   C. dropped out
   D. hung out

3. The teacher gave the students an interesting homework _____.
   A. assignment   B. dormitory   C. cafeteria
   D. professor

4. I'm going to have to _____ next week. I have a big exam coming soon.
   A. look forward to   B. have the hots for
   C. hit the books   D. pick on

5. Sarah likes to _____ with her friends at the shopping mall after school.
   A. hit the books   B. hang out   C. break up

D. drop out

6. Some people let off some _____ on the night of the festival.
A. music   B. rubbish   C. fireworks   D. snacks

7. The teacher was _____ by the student's high test score.
A. embarrassed   B. inspired   C. impressed
D. confused

8. David didn't know that Julie _____ him. He thought they were just friends.
A. picked on   B. gave up on   C. broke up with
D. had the hots for

9. After having a lot of trouble in their relationship, Jim and Sandy decided to _____.
A. break up   B. drop out   C. show off
D. break away

10. I don't think you should _____ going to the gym. It's great way to stay healthy.
A. drop out of   B. look forward to   C. give up
D. carry on

Appendix C: Mini-test answers & discussion questions

C-I. Mini-test answers
1. D
2. C
3. A
4. C
5. B
6. C
7. C
8. D
9. A
10. C

C-2. Discussion questions
1. What do you think will happen to Ria next in this story?

2. Have you ever had any experiences like Ria had in this story?

3. Have you ever entered a competition?

4. Do you think some people use smartphones too much?

5. What is something you would like to study in the future?

Try other books in the Breaking Free series

__Book 1__ Ria's first year at university is not going well. She has problems with her courses and her part-time job. But after an accident and a meeting with an international student, her life starts to change in surprising ways.

__Book 2__ Ria has some good times and some bad times at university. She makes some interesting new friends and has fun at a big music concert. But Ria has new problems. She gets some bad news and starts to worry about her future. She is also worried about her boyfriend, Lockie.

__Book 3__ Ria goes back to university after the holidays. She has problems with her best friend Shelly. She also has more trouble at the pizza shop. But Ria gets some good advice and decides to try making some changes. Can she change her ways? And what will happen with Shelly?

__Book 4__ Ria starts her second year at university. She is excited to find a new place to live and has a barbecue party with all her friends. But Ria is also busy with her part-time job and studying for exams. Can she still become a designer?

__Book 5__ Ria starts her final year at university. She enjoys a beach trip and watching a big rugby game with her friends. But Ria has trouble looking for a designer job. Then, she gets some help from a surprising place. How will Ria's university life end?

Cover photo: Konstantin Kolosov

Design and images: Geoff Macca

*Pomaka: Supporting English language learners and educators
For more publications and content related to language learning and teaching, visit our website at https://pomaka.com*

*Copyright © 2021 Paul McAleese
All rights reserved. No part of this book may be reproduced, stored in a retrieval system, or transmitted in any form by any means, electronic, mechanical, photocopying, recording or otherwise, without prior permission in writing from the author. This is a work of fiction. Any resemblance to actual people (living or dead), businesses, or events is purely coincidental.*

CPSIA information can be obtained
at www.ICGtesting.com
Printed in the USA
LVHW082332181222
735489LV00009B/965